THE MURDER

AT

THE

DEADWOOD

CASTLE

V.S ARAVINDH

For enquiry:
aravindhvs12@gmail.com

V.S ARAVINDH

*TO EVERYONE WHO
LOVES NOVELS….......*

CHAPTERS

INTRODUCTION

Detective James Faulkner has been haunted by tragedy and silence for fifteen years. But when a mysterious letter arrives with a coded message, it sparks the return of his sharp mind to solve a case that could change everything. Together with his loyal companion, William Shorteye, they embark on a dangerous journey to a distant town—only to find themselves in a race against time, where every second counts. With enemies unknown, and a secret waiting to be uncovered, Faulkner must navigate a web of puzzles, danger, and deception. Will he uncover the truth, or is this case too dangerous even for a man with his dark past?

CHAPTER 1
THE BEGINNING

The year was 1898. James Faulkner, a detective, was sipping on some tea, sitting on his shaking chair quietly in Old England. It was a calm, dark, and wet day, with some rainfall the previous night. He is a tall, quiet, and witty man who doesn't like to speak that much. Faulkner has got a dark history. 15 years ago, some burglar set his house on fire in the middle of the night back in New Hampshire, which killed his mom and his 3-year-old daughter.

He has a companion who is opposite to him - William Shorteye.

"A cold day, I reckon," said William.

"Sure, it is." Replied Faulkner.

"I have prepared the lunch, some delicious sausage and beans. So come and eat it before it gets too cold."

"You call that delicious, William? I wish I were at my old house back in New Hampshire, where my mother would have cooked me the full English meal." That housefire destroyed my life."

"Leave it, man, it was 15 years ago. I am sure your mom and daughter are in heaven smiling at you."

"I wish"

"You know, we haven't got a case in a year for us to solve, dear goodness me. The people will forget our wittiness"

"More like my wittiness, haha"

"You got tea for me, William?

"It's in the kitchen."

James and William both had dinner and took a small nap. Two hours later, they woke up to find mail at the front door.

CHAPTER 2

THE MYSTERIOUS LETTER

"Oh, look there James, a mail. We haven't received one in years, I reckon. Let me grab it asap."

Faulkner opened the mail and saw a series of codes written on it. Both of them were confused, but they got to work quickly.

XLNV GL SVOORMDLLW GLNLLLD NLIMRMT ZG VRTSG'L XOLXP. R DROO YV DZRGRMT ULI ZG GSV YZI

–FMPMLDM

"What in the world is this, James?"

He didn't reply as his mind was already locked in, at the code.

"What could this mean? I think the author is in trouble and begging us to help him/her. Do you have any idea, James?"

"It seems to be an alphabetic puzzle. I am pretty sure that there is a pattern in this. If we exchange the letters with the letter before or after it, it forms a senseless sentence. So, let's try to reverse the alphabet and see if we can decode it."

"What do you mean James?"

"See, in this method, the letter Z becomes A, the letter B becomes

Y, and so on. Bring me a notebook, Quick!"

His idea worked flawlessly. In the end, he ended up with this sentence.

'COME TO HELLINGWOOD TOMORROW MORNING AT EIGHT CLOCK. I WILL BE WAITING FOR YOU AT THE PUB'

– UNKNOWN

"Brilliant James, brilliant. Your wit hasn't rusted even after a year. But the mystery lies, who is the author of this?"

"We don't have time, William. We have to leave within an hour to catch the next train to Hellingwood."

"What's our plan

"I will tell you on the way. Pack your bags and get ready. We are off to an adventure after a whole year."

CHAPTER 3

THE JOURNEY TO HELLINGWOOD

As soon as they got ready, James Faulkner called his trusty taxi driver, Emmanuel to drop them at the railway station. He arrived in an old-fashioned white coloured car, which was visibly very worn out.

They reached the station and boarded the train to Hellingwood.

"Quite comfortable seats, aren't they James?"

"Don't be distracted. We should plan our next move. This train will reach the Hellingwood station at morning 7. 45. We have got only 15 minutes to get to the bar to meet the anonymous author."

"Don't worry about that. The bar is located just behind the station. So, we should be good. Anyway, do you fancy a game of chess?"

"It's been a long time since we last played chess. Bring it on!"

After the game, they set up their bed and drifted away, only to be wakened up by a tall, handsome figure, possibly in his thirties informing them that we were about to reach the Densington station.

"Densington? Isn't this the train to Hellingwood?

"Oh no, we will be passing through Hellingwood, but the

train will not stop there." Replied the gentleman.

"Goodness gracious me, we might have spoiled our entire plan. How are we going to meet him/her, James?

"We have to run as quickly as possible to reach the bar.

"Sir, do you know when we will pass through the Hellingwood Station?

 "We will reach the station in 30 seconds."

 "We have no other choice, but to jump off the train when I say so."

"Yes Sir"

"JUMP! William"

"Oh, ouch, that hurt"

"You okay, William?"

"Yeah"

"Quick, let's run to the bar"

"I don't think, I will be able to run. My legs are bleeding.'

"Oh no William, looks like I have to carry you now to the bar."

"It's 8.35. Please go to the bar as soon as possible. I shall crawl till I reach the bar. Run James, run."

James quickly ran out and saw the bar from a distance. Judging by its appearance and architectural style, it looked like it was at least a century old.

"I hope the author hasn't left" James murmured to himself.

He loaded his 1890 pistol just in case something went wrong and entered the bar.

There was no one there except for a shady-looking lady sitting in a dark corner of the room serving herself a large bottle of alcohol.

She was a tall woman, with long blonde hair with a distinct red mark on her chin.

James walked slowly toward the lady until the lady noticed him.

"Welcome, James Faulkner, to my bar. Would you like a drink or any snacks?

"Who are you, madam? Are you the person who sent us the letter yesterday?

"Sit down, James. I will tell you everything in a minute. Let your friend arrive first."

"How do you know that I have a companion?"

At that time, William arrived at the bar, Looking very much in pain.

"Come here my dear, I will treat you"

The lady then proceeded to cover his wound with bandages and covered it with medicine.

"How do you feel now?" Asked the lady.

"Fine"

James demanded the woman to tell them why she sent a code yesterday telling them to come here, and why was it written in a code rather than in proper English.

CHAPTER 4

SPEAKING WITH CATHERINE DEADWOOD

"I am Catherine Deadwood, the youngest of the 2 daughters of Sir Joseph Deadwood. We used to be a rich family back in the Netherlands. The location of our wealth is a closely kept secret known only to my father.

He died 15 years ago, in 1883, due to a heart attack, without being able to share the location of our wealth.

A few days ago, my sister-Juliana Deadwood died mysteriously in the mansion. I don't know how that happened.

So, I hired many detectives to investigate this, but all of them rejected. This is why, I am resorting to you, sir.

The letter, which I sent you yesterday was a test to see if you are capable of doing this. Well, you have passed the test.

Are you willing to help me?"

"Sure, mam"

"James, does that mean we have to go to the Netherlands."

"Yeah"

"It's going to be super expensive."

"Don't worry you two, I will bear your expenses. We can leave tomorrow itself."

"What is our plan"

"Today evening, we will depart from the railway station to London. From there we will catch a train to Margate. Then, we will be boarding the 'Dutch Queen' which will take us to The Hague. And finally, we will take a train, which will take us to Deadwood."

"Oh Wow, the place is named after your family." Said William.

"My Great-Great-Great grandfather- Sir Charles Deadwood named this place in the year 1267"

"Really?"

"Madam, I have got a few questions to ask."

"Sure, go on"

"Has anyone entered the mansion after her death other than you?

"Only the mortician entered the mansion to collect her body"

"Have you found any items that could have been used to kill her?

"No, but I found some hair, which I think is hers. It was found just near her body. We made sure that we didn't disturb the hair so that you could come and see"

"Were there any marks on her body?"

"Well, I didn't check that"

"Has the body been buried?

"No, her body is kept at the mortician's office."

"Great. We will be able to check if there are any injuries or scars on her body. Any sketch on how she was lying on the ground"

"No"

"No problem. Is there anyone in the mansion right now?

"Yes, the 2 security guards. But they have been ordered not to enter the mansion."

"Did you hear anything breaking on that night?"

"No."

"Noted, madam"

"Do you fancy a cup of beer?"

"We don't drink but, we will enjoy a delicious breakfast."

"Follow me to my temporary home. I have prepared the full

English Breakfast just for you two."

The three of them had their breakfast and decided to take a nap, as they were tired from the travel the previous day. But after some time, the three of them started feeling nauseous and lightheaded.

"James, I am not feeling well"

"Me too, I am feeling nauseous. Where is Catherine?

"There she is. Wait, she is also vomiting."

"I think, we got food poisoning gentlemen. I think I have the medicines for this. Here, have this."

Thirty minutes passed, and they started feeling better.

"What just happened to us? I prepared the food, just in the morning. There is no way, that the food got bad in just an hour."

"Did someone try to poison us?" Wondered William.

"Is there a lab nearby?" Asked James.

"Yes, there is one just down the street. Let us take the sample of our food and head there."

CHAPTER 5: THE VISIT TO THE PHARMACIST

They reached the pharmacist's office. But there was no one there. They rang the bell over 5 times until there was a response. A short, dark-skinned lady with curly hair wearing a green apron opened the door. She welcomed us in and asked why we had come here.

James Faulkner explained everything and gave the sample to the pharmacist.

"Lady, may I ask, what is your name?"

"Oh, I am Emilia."

"Nice to meet you,"

"Oh thanks, William!"

"It will take about 20 minutes to examine this. I will try to finish this as soon as possible and issue the report"

"You can take your own time," said William, blushing.

Emilia quickly went to the lab and started working on it.

"Hey James, I have something to tell you"

"What is it?"

"I think I am in love with her"

"Oh, that's nice, but this is not the time to get romantic, William. We have to be serious. We are dealing with a murder case."

"Okay, sorry," said William with a heavy heart.

That's when Catherine said something concerning.

"Gentlemen, I don't know why, but I feel like someone is watching us right now in a distance."

"Really?"

"Yeah. Should I go and check? I am getting an eerie feeling."

"Not. I reckon no one will be able to watch us, as there are no windows around us. It could be your brain playing tricks with you. It could be possibly due to the food poisoning too." Replied James.

But unbeknownst to them, Catherine's eerie feeling was true. Someone, unknown to them was watching their every move through the cracks in the wall. Someone, with sinister thoughts.........

Within 15 minutes, they received the results and it sent shivers down their spines. Someone had poured Mercury into the meal. This could have caused Mercury poisoning which could lead to their death. Luckily, the mercury content wasn't that high, and that saved their lives.

"My lord! I can't believe we survived after consuming Mercury." Exclaimed William

"There is surely someone behind this attempted murder. But who could this be? This surely can't be Catherine, as she ate it, and became sick. No one would ever do that knowing the consequences of Mercury poisoning."

"But, why would anyone even want to murder us in the first place?" Asked William.

"That's the thing, we don't know. But I have a crazy theory. I think the person responsible for the murder of   Juliana Deadwood is aware of our plan and is trying to murder us."

"That can't be possible James. I left the Netherlands in secrecy. Not even my relatives know that I am in England." Said Catherine.

"See lady, a person who is crazy enough to murder someone is also crazy enough to follow someone in secrecy to see their plans. I have a suspicion that the same person is listening to us right now" Replied James.

"Oh lord, please save us"

"Thank you, Emilia, for helping us. Your help is invaluable. Right now, we are in a hurry. We have to leave for London in 30 minutes."

"You are welcome, gentlemen"

CHAPTER 6:

HELLINGWOOD TO DEADWOOD

"Gentlemen, we have to get to the station as soon as possible. The train will reach the station in 8 minutes according to the schedule."

"Detectives are always ready."

"Good. Let us then leave for the station."

As soon as they reached the station, they boarded the train, and in 5 minutes the train departed the Hellingwood Station.

"Mam, when will we reach the Deadwood station?"

"It would take us about 4 days."

"So, we will reach the Deadwood station on Christmas Eve- 24 December 1898." Said William.

"Yeah."

"James, what is your plan?"

"As we, will reach Deadwood on 24 December, I reckon we can visit the mansion and the mortician's office on 25th December at dawn."

"Ok"

It was a silent and smooth journey till Watford, where the train came to a dead stop.

"Oh goodness gracious, I was about to fall. How do you both remain calm and composed?" Asked Catherine.

"A true detective is always alert of his surroundings."

"But what happened right now? Why did we come to a dead stop in the middle of England?"

By then, the train supervisor came to our compartment and explained that someone installed a grenade in the engine causing it to blow up. He also added that it would take 6 hours for the replacement train to arrive as the train is currently at the Edinburg Central Station.

"Oh no! It seems like we will be missing our next train" Exclaimed Catherine.

James and William could see the desperation in her eyes.

"Sir, I am a detective. Shall I check the bomb which was detonated?"

"Sure"
William joined James
reluctantly to check the train
engine.

"Are you sure we have to do
this?" asked William

"Yes. I reckon this could give us
a hint on the murder."

"How?"

"Time will tell.

Oh, look there, I think they are
the fragments of the bomb.
Indeed it is."

"What is written on that?"

"Let me see. I reckon it is
written 'MADE IN
DEADWOOD'

"That's the place that we are
going to!"

"Quick! Give me a bag. We have to store the fragments. It could be a big lead in our murder case. I reckon, there could be more of these bombs in the train. We have to inform Catherine and the train supervisor."

They quickly entered the train and informed Catherine and the train supervisor. Catherine was visibly distressed after hearing this.

Richard- The train supervisor permitted them to check the entire train for bombs.

"We can start from the first compartment to the last. There are a total of 24 compartments in this train."

"I would be happy to help you," said Catherine.

"That's great. So, if you find any bomb, just throw it away at a safe distance from the train and then collect the remaining after it explodes in this bag. I am pretty sure that it will help us in the murder case."

The 3 of them searched all of the compartments but didn't find a single bomb at the end.

"That's strange. I reckon there is more than 1 on this train. Did anyone search our compartment,

"No"

"No"

"Let me search.

OH GOODNESS ME! There is a bomb right under our seat. Quick, let me detonate it."

James threw the bomb out, detonated it, and collected the fragments in separate bags.

"The sentence 'MADE IN DEADWOOD' is written on the bomb too. Someone is behind this assassination attempt. Someone is trying to assassinate us. Everyone should be on their guard from now on."

"Yes sir"

"Richard, when will the replacement train arrive?"

"In about 4 hours."

"Where has it reached?"

"Lockerbie"

"At this rate, we will surely miss our next train. Catherine, when will our train from London to Margate depart?"

"Tomorrow at 11 pm"

"Let's just pray that we will reach in time."

2 hours passed, and with each passing second, the 3 of them were getting stressed. The rest of the passengers were also stressed out, and some started revolting.

"Oh no, the people are starting to get violent. How are you gentlemen not bothered at all by these visuals?" Exclaimed Catherine.

"We have seen much worse things than this." Replied William in a nonchalant way.

Another hour passed and there were no signs of the train.

"Sir, when will our train arrive? We are getting late for our connecting train."

"Sir, it has reached Cambridge. It should reach here in 1 hour."

"It should."

Right then, the compartment blew up. The people in the compartment were killed instantly except for a few. The survivors included James, William, Catherine, and a few others. Richard didn't survive……

"Oh lord, what was that?" exclaimed William.

"How did we survive?" wondered Catherine.

"This is a full-fledged war against us. Someone is trying to kill us but failed both times.

Looks like we have failed to retrieve all the bombs."

"Ahh, I am bleeding profusely. Someone, please help me." cried a stranger.

Before they could help him, he had uttered his last words. The people from the other compartments ran towards us and helped us. They carried away the dead bodies and burnt them. Catherine couldn't sustain the injuries and fainted.

The people carried her to the next compartment and laid her down and tried to wake her up.

James and William were pretty shaken up by the incident.

"Did we lose her?" asked Williams

"No, she is still breathing. She is okay."

"Thank goodness"

By then, the replacement train had arrived. It took us a long time to explain what happened, to the crew members. They were pretty distressed after hearing this. James told the crew members to be alert and aware of their surroundings. After everyone boarded the train, the train departed. To make up for the loss of time, they added an extra 20 kg of coal and increased the speed. They were going at 51 km per hour which was very dangerous. About half an hour later, Catherine woke up from her coma.

Everyone stayed alert and nobody was able to sleep

thinking about the incident and the people who died.

Nonetheless, the journey was smooth and they reached London the next day half an hour late.

"I still can't believe that we survived the explosion yesterday."

"We were seated at the back and the explosion occurred at the front of the compartment. That is how we got away with that."

"Close. I think it was an accident"

"It was not an accident. It was a failed assassination attempt. I highly suspect that the person behind your sister's murder is also behind this. Anyway, when will our train to Margate arrive?"

"I reckon, it will arrive in 30 minutes or so."

"How long will it take us to reach Margate?

"About 8 hours."

"Okay. Everyone should be alert. We don't know if anyone is still trying to kill us."

"How are you so sure that someone is trying to kill us?"

"It's my instincts."

"Well, I hope it is not true and just our bad luck"

"I hope" added Catherine

Within 20 minutes the train arrived, and they boarded the train. They made sure to tell the explosion incident to the train supervisor and managed to get permission to search the train. This was a much smaller train with 15 compartments. This time, James checked all the compartments and found no bombs or any weapons whatsoever. He was relieved but not assured.

"I have not found any bombs in the compartments or the engine."

"I reckon we are safe, right?"

"I can't assure you."

"Why?" asked Catherine.

"Because the person we are dealing with, is a mastermind. It seems like he is experienced in these things."

"Why do you say so?"

"You should understand it yourselves."

The 3 of them sat down at their seats, but it was very visible that the 3 of them were visibly distressed thinking about the dangers that loomed before them. But now it is too late to abort the missions as their train has departed the London Central Station for the Margate Station.

They had not eaten a morsel since yesterday as they had lost their appetite after that mercury poisoning.

It was a quiet journey until they reached Maidstone. A long sharp arrow targeted toward the window hit Catherine's shoulder. They understood that this was again an attempt to take their life.

"Ahhh! Lord!" screamed Catherine.

"Yet again! Close all of the windows, quick!"

Right then, another arrow narrowly missed James's skull.

"Goodness gracious me! James, are you all, right?"

"Yeah, I am. Check on Catherine. Is she breathing?"

"Thank goodness she is."

"Someone bring the first aid, quick!"

"Here it is."

A young teen, possibly 16, gave them the first aid box and provided some water for Catherine. It took a long time for Catherine to wake. But thankfully, she was alright.

"Are you all right, mam? Asked the young man.

"Yeah, but it is paining severely. Ahh"

"Don't worry madam. Here have some water."

"What's your name, gentleman?" Asked James.

"I am Rudolf Deadwood."

"WHAT! You both share the same last name. Where are your parents, young man?

"Sir, I am an orphan. I remember being dropped off on the streets of Deadwood 16 years ago by my mother. But I don't remember her name or how she looks."

"Wait a second, young man. I will get to you in a bit."

"Catherine, do you have a son?"

"Yes. 17 years back, I was pregnant with a young boy. But when my husband knew it, he was furious as he wanted a girl. He made me abandon him on the streets of Darkwood. I have never met him after that." She said, with tears in her eyes.

"Well, I have a shocking news."

"What is it?"

"The young man who helped you is your son. His name is Rudolph Deadwood."

RUDOLPH!? He is my son. Where is he?"

Right then Rudolph who heard all of this came running to

Catherine. The duo hugged each other and started crying.

"My son. I am sorry. I had no choice, but to listen to your arrogant father."

"Don't worry Mother, I forgive you."

With a teary eye and a happy face, William said; "Happiness at last. She has forgotten that she is wounded. That is the power of love, I tell you, James."

"True."

The duo had a great conversation and then told him everything that happened in the last few days. She also asked him, if he would like to join the. He agreed without any hesitation.

Then, James asked him a few questions.

"Young man, how were you able to sustain yourself for 17 years?"

"Sir, it's a very long story. After she abandoned me, I stayed in the casket for 2 days straight without any food or water. Then a gentleman saw me lying on the ground and decided to adopt me. And that changed my life. I reckon we lived at Deadwood for 2 years before moving to England When I was 4, I was sent to a private school. I was very good at studies and cricket. I was selected in the U-13 Cricket team at 12. I ended up winning the player of the tournament and that earned me 1000 pounds.

My talent was recognized by the England Cricket Board and I was selected in the national team last year."

"Oh, congrats my boy. Anyhow, where are you going to?" William asked.

"Oh, I am going to Deadwood to meet my old friends."

"Oh nice, I am sure your mom told you, but we are also going to Deadwood."

"Yeah, I know."

"Also, be careful of your surroundings. You never know what danger lies in front of you."

"Yes sir."

"Good."

"Catherine, how many more hours left before we reach the Margate Station?"

"About 3 hours."

"Good."

"Tomorrow once we reach the Margate station, we have to buy bulletproof jackets and other supplies just in case something goes wrong."

"Ok, sir."

"And Rudolph, you are not allowed to come with us."

"Why sir?"

"You are just 17 years old and have a bright career in cricket. We don't want to risk your life."

"But sir, I want to be with my mother."

"It's dangerous Rudolph. Please understand it."

"Ok, sir. Anyway, I reckon you all are hungry from the travel and the adventure, right?"

"Yeah," said William.

"I have got some leftovers with me. You can have it."

"Thank you, young man, for providing us with food. We hadn't eaten anything since yesterday."

"You welcome Sir."

"Well, I think, we are free of danger now as all the windows have been closed and I have checked for the bombs. So, anyone up for a game of chess, maybe?"

"I am up for it"

"Good"

The game lasted for 3 hours and it ended as a draw due to insufficient material.

"Wonderful game of chess, I must say. Well, I am happy that I have got a new companion to play chess with."

"Gentlemen, we have reached the Margate Station right on time."

"Good. When is our ferry scheduled to depart?"

"Tomorrow 6.00 am"

"What is the time now?"

"7.30 pm."

"I reckon we have about 10 and ½ hours left. Have you booked a hotel?

"Yes. It is right behind the station."

"Good."

"Well Rudolph, let's play a game once we reach the room."

"Sure."

After they reached their room, they locked all the doors and windows. They checked for bombs or any other weapons which could be used to kill them.

"Have you closed all the windows, son?" asked Catherine.

"Yeah."

"I don't want to risk our life yet again. That was a close one on the train. If it had hit my neck, then I reckon it would have been the end for me."

"Sir, can we play a game of chess?

"Sure. Try to beat me this time."

"Okay, sir."

This time the game took 4 and ½ hours and it was still a draw.

"A perfect game of chess always ends in a draw!" exclaimed James.

"True."

"Okay, it's time for us to sleep. It's midnight and our ferry is scheduled to depart at 6 am."

"Ok, sir. Good night."

They had a good night's sleep and arrived at the seaport early in the morning. As soon as they arrived, they went straight to the pilot's cabin to get his permission to search the ferry for any explosives. But this time the pilot didn't allow him saying that it was just stupidity.

"No sir. We are telling the truth. Someone is behind us trying to get us killed. You would regret this if you don't allow us."

"I reckon you all are drunk. We conduct security checks before every trip. So please just go back to your seat and sit quietly."

"I have only one thing to say, if my predictions are true, then you are in big trouble."

"Sure."

Right then, a worker came running and said- "Sir, we have found a huge bomb."

"WHAT!?" replied the captain.

"Where did you find it?" Asked William.

"It was lying near the engines."

"What was written on it?"

"I reckon it was written- 'MADE IN DEADWOOD and a 6-digit number."

"QUICK! Send as many people as possible to search for the bombs. Call a professional bomb diffuser too."

"Don't worry about that. I will take care of it."

The ship was then delayed by 2 hours due to checking, which made the people mad. Due to this, they started revolting. So, the pilot had to depart in the middle of searching.

"These people don't understand it until they experience it themselves." Muttered James.

"Catherine, when will we reach the Hague?"

"We were supposed to reach the 'The Hague' port tomorrow at 1 pm. But due to the delay, I think we will reach at 3 pm."

"No problem."

"James, I am feeling seasick." Said William.

"Why didn't you tell us that you suffer from seasickness back at Margate? We would have bought some medicines for seasickness for you."

"Don't worry sir. I have some lemons as well as a few tablets for sea sickness."

"You are my hero!" Exclaimed William.

"Ah, thanks, sir."

"I am feeling a bit dizzy and tired, so I am going to take a nap." Said William with a weak voice.

"Ok"

Before long, they had their food and then took a nap, only to be woken up by the attendants. They informed me that they would reach the seaport in 2 minutes. And no one was happier than William.

"Finally, land! Have we reached Deadwood?"

"No. We still have one more train journey left."

"Oh no!"

"What is the time right now?

"It's currently 3.10 pm. Our next train will depart from The Hague Central Railway station at 4 pm. So, we have to hurry up."

"Quick, call a taxi to the railway station." Ordered James.

Within 10 minutes, the taxi arrived and they arrived at the station.

"There is our train. Let's board on that beauty." Said Rudolph.

"Rudolph"

"Yes sir."

"As soon as you reach Deadwood, you can stay at your friend's house as you intended to at the beginning of your journey. Don't come with us as it's dangerous."

"Ok, sir."

"William, close all the windows. We are going to check the train."

This train was the smallest of the 3 in which they had traveled. It had only 8 compartments. After checking, he informed James that he had found none."

"Good. I reckon he is off our trail now." Said James.

"I hope so."

The train departed 30 minutes late but they reached Deadwood almost 10 minutes earlier.

CHAPTER 7:
THE DEADWOOD CASTLE

"Finally, the traveling is over." Exclaimed William

"Where do we stay tonight?"

"At the palace."

"WHAT!? We are sleeping at the murder scene?" asked William

"Yeah"

"Where is the mortician's office?"

"It is about 5 km away from the palace."

"Good. We will visit the mortician's office tomorrow morning to examine her body.

Anyway Catherine, call the taxi to drop us at the palace."

"Sure."

Soon, the taxi arrived. When they entered the taxi, the driver smirked at Catherine and Catherine smirked back. James saw this but kept mum.

"Mm, suspicious." He thought to himself.

Within 20 minutes, they reached the mansion.

"Smaller than I expected!" exclaimed William.

"I reckon this is going to make the investigation easier."

"Yeah."

"Come inside, gentlemen. I will guide you to your room." Said Catherine.

"The mansion is so eerie and silent." Commented William.

"Catherine, if I remember correctly, you said that 2 security guards are standing at the gates of the mansion. Where are they?"

"I reckon they are in the mansion."

"But, back at Hellingwood, during the interrogation, I reckon that you said that you have ordered them to not enter the mansion, right?"

"Did I?"

"Yes, you did."

"I think they are probably in the back of the mansion."

"Let's check."

"No need James. You both are probably really tired from the traveling and the near-death experiences. You should probably take a nap."

"Yeah James, let us take a nap."

"Catherine, I have a condition."

"Go on."

"We will not sleep here. Rather, we will sleep at a nearby hotel, and then come tomorrow to investigate."

"Why?" asked Catherine.

James didn't reply. Rather he signed William to follow him to a nearby hotel.
"Where are we going, James?"

"To a nearby hotel."

"Why."

"I will tell you after we reach our hotel."

Within 10 minutes, they reached a hotel and they booked one room for 5 days. After they entered their room, they locked all the windows and doors covered all the cracks in the walls with cloth, and turned off all lights.

"Why are we doing this? Asked William.

"Shh! Speak quietly." Whispered James.

"Okay. Now tell me why we booked a separate hotel other than just staying in a room at the castle."

"I am quite suspicious of Catherine. Remember how she stuttered when I asked a few questions back at the gate of the mansion.?'

"Yeah. So, are you thinking that she is probably a fraud?"

"No."

"Then?"

"My instincts tell me that something bad will happen to us either at the castle or the mortuary."

"Nothing bad will happen."

"I hope so."

"I am going to take a nap now. I am really tired from the traveling."

"Me too. But be alert. Anything bad can happen here."

"Oh, sure." Replied William in a tired voice.

William slept for 5 hours before being woken up by his rumbling stomach.

"Good -evening James. Had a good nap, I reckon?"

"Yeah, I slept for 2 hours. Aren't you hungry by now?"

"How do you know."

"Just my instincts. Here, I brought a sandwich for the 2 of us."

"Cheers, James!"

"Cheers!"

They had their food and spent some time reading.

"What is the time now, William?"

"It's 7.25 pm."

"Date?"

"December 24"

"You realize, that tomorrow is Christmas, right?"

"Jesus Christ! I forgot due to traveling and those near-death experiences."

"Me too."

"I wish we were back at Old England. We would have been able to celebrate Christmas peacefully rather than risking our life multiple times to solve a murder case." Said, William

"I agree with you."

"Anyway William, give me the bag in which the bomb fragments were kept."

"Here it is."

"Do you have a magnifying glass by any chance?"

"Yes."

"Excellent."

"Here it is."

He searched the fragments of the bomb for any other small texts but was disappointed when there were none.

"Nothing other than 'MADE IN DEADWOOD' is written on it. Wait a second. There is a number written over here. 270125"

"How will we find who made this bomb if there is no marking on the bomb?"

"I am highly suspicious of Catherine. I think she is the person who is trying to kill us."

"But that doesn't make sense. If she tried to kill us, why would she even try to bring us here?

She could have killed us at Hellingwood itself. Moreover, she too suffered in all of the incidents. And Rudolph has recognized her as his mother who had abandoned him 17 years back."

"Great justification, William. My theory could be wrong, but I am still suspicious of her."

"Why do you say so?"

"When we entered the taxi after leaving the Darkwood station, I saw her smirking an evil smile at the driver. More the driver showed her a thumbs up with an evil smile."

"So?"

"So, my instincts say that something fishy is going on

behind our backs and beyond our understanding."

"Any solid proofs?"

"Yes. In- fact many."

"List them out, James."

"I will tell you later."

"Why are you always like this"

"I like to keep it as a suspense."

"Yeah, sure." Said William who was unhappy with his theory.

CHAPTER 8:

THE INVESTIGATION

William and James left their room and reached the castle at 7 in the morning. They saw Catherine waiting for them at the gate. There were also 2 security guards standing at the gate.

"Welcome back James. Good morning and a Merry Christmas"

"Well, this Christmas will not be merry. Anyway, good morning."

"Let us start the investigation." Said, William

"Come inside."

As they entered the mansion, they saw the interior walls to be covered with Black Mold.

"Uhh, black mold!" exclaimed William.

"Well, this castle is a really old one right."

"When was it made? Asked William.

"I reckon it was in the year 536

"It is not important William. Catherine, where was the body of Juliana found?"

"In the first floor."

"Take us there."

"Sure"

As they were climbing the stairs, one of the wooden plates on the stairs broke all of a sudden. This surprised James and William but not Catherine.

"What just happened right now?"

"Don't worry, this palace just needs some renovation. Let us move on."

"The whole castle has to be renovated"

"Yeah, there it is. That's the place where I found her body exactly 15 days ago."

"William, give me my glasses and my notebook."

"Here it is."

"Thanks."

Then, James started examining the things that were near the sight.

"There is absolutely nothing here except for a strand of hair just like you said back at Hellingwood. I am going to examine the entire castle for some evidence. William, store this hair in a bag."

"Sure."

'Let's start from the ground floor."

"Ok"

"Catherine, how many floors are in this mansion?"

"Only 2, the ground floor and the First floor."

"Good."

After they climbed down the stairs carefully, they started their investigation. They wrote down everything that probably could have used in some way on that fateful day.

"Nothing too concerning yet."

"Let us now investigate the first floor." William said

"Wait, we forgot to check the kitchen."

"Oh yeah."

When they entered the kitchen, they saw something shocking. They saw the glass pieces from the window scattered across the entire room.

"Catherine, was this window broken when you first found Juliana's body?"

"Yes."

"Then, why didn't you report this to me back at Hellingwood?

"I am sorry James; I had forgotten about this."

"Clumsy." He whispered to himself.

"Then let us check the first floor."

"Ok."

James didn't find anything worthy of clues on the first floor.

"I reckon that the criminal had entered the mansion through the back of the kitchen by breaking the window. But I have one question. Judging by the looks of it, I am sure that the murderer had broken it with a strong force. But, how didn't you hear the sound of glass breaking on that night?"

"I heard it."

"Lies. When I interrogated you back at Hellingwood, you said that you heard absolutely nothing on that night."

"Did I?"

"Here is the proof."

He showed the notebook in which he had noted her answers.

"Moreover, if you had heard something break, any normal person would check it out instead of just sleeping. But you said that you saw her body in the morning."

"I was too tired on that day, so I didn't bother myself checking it out."

"Sure. William, document everything that she said."

"Okay."

"Why? Don't you trust me?"

"I reckon it may provide us a clue about the murder."

"How?"

"You will see it in a short due of time."

"Let us move on to the first floor then."

"Okay"

"Be careful. I reckon this mansion needs a complete renovation. Catherine, was this mansion ever abandoned?"

"No, our family used to live here for more than a thousand years."

"Has anyone ever renovated this mansion?"

"I don't think so."

"Mm, okay."

"So, this is the place where the dead body was found right?"

"Mhm."

"No blood stains on the floor."

"No blood stains or injuries in the body too." Added Catherine.

"Hair found on the floor. Maybe an assault. No weapons were found. I conclude that this is possibly a case of strangling. But then, there should be a mark on her neck." Concluded William.

"Good. But don't conclude now. We still have to examine the body and the other rooms." Said James.

"Ok."

"Hey look over there, is that a dress?" asked William.

"Sure, it is."

"I think it could be possibly Juliana. Is it Juliana's room?"

"No"

"Then how could this be here?"

"Was she stripped before being strangled by the murderer?"

"No. She was covered when I found her body in the morning." Said Catherine with an anxious voice.

"Mm, okay. Note down everything. Also, take a small piece of that dress."

"Okay, James."

"Okay William, it seems that we have investigated the entire mansion. Now, the only place left is the backyard."

"Is it really necessary gentlemen? We have concluded that she had been strangled to death."

"Yes, it is indeed necessary. It could give additional clues on the murderer's identity." Said William.

"I think we are wasting our time searching this house. Let us go to the mortuary to check on the dead body." Said Catherine

"What seems to be the problem here, lady? Why are you in such a hurry? Why, are you missing your beloved sister?" asked James.

"Nothing"

"Yeah, let us go, William."

"Sure."

"Be careful. These steps are super scary."

"Ok, sir."

"Oh lord, this place needs a renovation."

"True."

James saw that Catherine was tensed as they were getting close to the backyard. But as they reached the backyard, James could see that she was now calm. By now, James had started to suspect Catherine.

"There is nothing here." Concluded Catherine.

"Are you sure?"

"Yes. Let us now leave for the mortuary."

As they were leaving, James saw a key which by appearance

looked quite old dangling on the tree branch. He secretly took the key without anyone knowing kept then in his coat and then headed off to the mortuary along with Catherine and William.

They reached the mortuary in 10 minutes. The building appeared to have been built in the 13th century. It was completely worn out and James wondered how this could have been possibly ever used as a mortuary. He also realized that there were no windows or doors other than the front door. He also realized that there was no graveyard behind or anywhere close to the mortuary.

"Quite an odd building I reckon"

"Sure, it is. I reckon it was built way back in the 13th century."
Said, William

"Do you mind if I ask you a question?"

"Go on."

"Most mortuaries have a graveyard behind them. But there seems to be none here. Are there any?"

"Oh, I do not know about this."

"Does the mortician know me or William."

"I don't think so."

"Sure, you don't," said James concerned.

"Let us enter then."

"Mm, okay."

"Where's the body stored?"

"I don't know. We have to ask the mortician."

"Where is he?"

"Mr. Rutherford, where are you?"

"Here I am mam, wait a second."

"Sure, take your time."

"Mr. Rutherford met them after a while. Mr. Rutherford was a tall man, with curly hair and was eerily similar to Catherine."

"Are you related by any chance?"

"Oh no. We are not." Replied Mr. Rutherford.

"I reckon I have seen you somewhere. Anyway sir, what do have to comment on the body? Are there any marks or bruises or anything on her body? Or has she been poisoned?"

"I have found a couple of bruises on her neck. There are no possibilities of poisoning."

"How are you so sure sir?"

"Listen here, James. I am an experienced mortician. I know what I am doing and you don't need to learn more."

"Oh, I am sorry sir. Reckon that you are in a bad mood. Anyway, sir, I have a question for you. How do you know my name? Catherine had told us that you do not know us."

"It is not important."

"It IS important."

"You know what is more important? Doing your job."

"Where is her body being stored?" asked James in a furious tone.

James was frustrated with the mortician and his way of talking.

"Right inside that room. I will lead you there."

Right as they reached the entrance, something flashed through James's mind.

"Hey Catherine, you had told me that your sister was murdered 15 days ago, right?"

"Yeah, what about it?"

"On average a human body decomposes in about 10 days. There is no way her body is preserved. These medicines are not capable of preserving a body this long."

"I don't know anything about this thing. Better ask Mr. Rutherford about this."

"Why don't you both just check the body yourselves? Your questions will be answered."

"Yeah, come on James, let us check it." Said William.

CHAPTER 9:

TRAPPED

Right as they entered, a large wall made of iron fell which blocked the way out for William and James.

"What happened James?" asked William with a face of terror.

"We have been TRICKED! Tricked from Old England to Hellingwood to London to Margate to The Hague to the infamous Deadwood Castle. Why didn't I realize that this was a trick? Right as she said that she was murdered 15 days ago, I should have realized that it was a TRICK. I am an idiot."

Said James with agony on his face.

"What will we do now?"

Right then, Catherine opened a small vent from the other side and started talking.

"Well, well, well, guess who is here! The best detective on the planet Earth has fallen for our mouse trap. Hahahaha!"

"Shut up you monster!" yelled William.

"What if I don't? Hahahaha?"

"Lady, tell me everything in detail. Why did you capture us? Why did you create the characters? Why?"

"Calm down, detective. I will tell you everything. First, please let us celebrate in peace."

She then abruptly closed the vent.

"We are doomed." Said, William

"I hope not."

"Check, if we have anything to break open the door." Said William.

"Not now. Even if we did, I am pretty sure that they have a trick up their sleeves. So, remain quiet and listen to what they are saying."

William and James both pressed their ears to the wall to hear what they were speaking. But unfortunately, right at that time, 'Catherine' opened the went and saw them in their act.

"Oh well, I expected this. Don't worry mate. I shall tell you everything tomorrow morning."

"Tomorrow morning!? Tell us right now, you demoness."

"Mind your words, James. I will kill you right now if you don't shut your stupid mouth."

James and William both remained quiet after that.

"Mm, Hahaha. Good job. You seem to understand everything other than my tricks. Anyway, I am locking this door and I will only open this tomorrow morning."

"What about food?" asked William

"Food? Ha, I wouldn't even give you a single morsel of bread.

 Now, have a great day." Catherine said sarcastically.

'What will we do now? We are doomed." Said William while crying bitterly.

"Stop crying, James. You are 42. I am sure we will be able to escape.'

"How?"

"Somehow. Now, go and take a nap. She is not going to open this door or feed us until tomorrow."

Both of them took a nap and woke up a few hours later.

"What is the time now, James?"

"How would I know? There are no windows or clocks here. I also forgot to change the London time to the Deadwood time."

"Yeah, let us try to hear what they are saying."

"I reckon the sound which I am hearing right now is the sound of them both snoring."

"I then reckon that it is nighttime right now."

"Yeah, or they are taking a nap during the daytime, or it is just one of their tricks once again."

"Do you have any food on you mate? I am starving."

"No William."

"I am going to check the entire room for anything that we can use to get out of here."

"I don't think that there would be any."

"How are you so sure about that James?"

"See, those demons have carefully prepared the plan and

have executed it perfectly to bring us to Deadwood from Old London. There is no way that they are going to give us a clue to get out of here."

"I reckon you are right mate, but I still want to check this out."

"As you wish, William. Do whatever you want."

The search was over within a few minutes as the room in which they were locked was small.

"You were right James. There is absolutely nothing here. Are we doomed forever?"

"I hope not. I am curious as to why she captured us. If she wanted to kill us, I reckon she could have done it back at Hellingwood."

"There were multiple attempts on our life James. Remember the bomb explosions, the mercury poisoning, the attack with arrows, and much more."

"In all of those incidents, the 'Catherine' was the person who suffered the most. This is why I did not suspect her. Your suspicions were right, William, you were right." Said James with a low and sad tone.

"I reckon this is our fate to suffer and die in this mortuary."

"This is not a mortuary."

"Why do you say so?"

"It is quite obvious for you to understand that this is not a mortuary. First of all, there is no graveyard behind or anywhere near this building. Secondly, there are no rooms in this building which can be used to store the bodies. We are stuck in the room which we thought was the place where the bodies are stored. And it is quite obvious that 'Rutherford' is not a mortician. Everything is staged."

"Does that mean that Juliana and Rudolph are also fake?"

"Yes. I reckon that these people are working as a family to capture us. But the one thing that I can't comprehend is why would they even want to capture us in the first place. Are there any dark motives behind their plans? I don't know. Sigh."

"Ahh, I am starving."

"Me too. I wish she at least gave us a piece of bread."

"Yeah. I am just going to take a nap yet again."

Both of them again took a nap and they woke up in the morning. But the problem is that both of them, don't have any idea about the time.

"What do you reckon the time is right now?"

"Probably 8 am. I can hear some birds chirping outside this horrific building. But I can't seem to hear the voices of 'Catherine' and 'Rutherford'."

"Have they tricked us into living in this room for the rest of our lives?"

"Probably. Let us wait for them"

"Yeah, sure. That is the only thing that we can do now."

1 hour passed. No one.

2 hours passed. No one.

5 hours passed. No one.

8 hours passed. No one.

By this time, James and William started going crazy due to starvation, dehydration, and anxiety. They were starting to hallucinate to which at one point William thought that they were back at Old London.

"Hey James, we are back in London."

"Really? I thought we were in New Hampshire."

It took them 2 hours before they were back to their old self.

"Oh, stop dreaming. We are still in the room." Wake up, William, wake up.

"Oh hey, sweetheart."

"This man has gone crazy," James muttered to himself.

James slapped him in the face and that did the job.

"Why would you slap me, James?"

"I tried waking you up. But you wouldn't. That is why I resorted to violence."

"Are we safe now?"?

"Look around you. Does it look like we are out of here?"

"No. Does that mean we are stuck here until we die?"

"If we find our way out, then not." Said James.

"That is it. I am going to break open the door. I want fresh air. I want to be free." Screamed William.

"Have you gone crazy? This door is made of strong iron and other materials. You can't possibly do that without the help of a hammer or anything."

"I don't care."

"You will probably break your hand doing that."

"Right."

James was happy that he finally persuaded him to not do that.

"But do something to get us out of here. Don't just sit there doing nothing."

"What am I supposed to do?"

"Search for any code or anything like that on the door or the walls or floor or anywhere to get us out."

"Ok. But the thing is, this room is extremely dark. I can't even see your face."

"Use your senses,"

"Whatever."

"After 10 minutes of searching, he found absolutely nothing.

"I told you, William. There will be nothing inside this dark room that will help us escape. They are incredibly smart. I feel this is not the first time they have done something like this. They are highly experienced in this scam."

"Nooo. We are doomed."

"No, we are not. We can do something to escape."

"What can you do?"

"Let me think."

"Sure. Take your time. But please, I want to go out."

"Mm, okay."

"For the next 2 and a half hours, James kept on roaming the room deep in thought. He didn't reply whenever William called as he wasn't able to hear him. At last, James said something disappointing.

"We are stuck here until our death."

"WHAT?! D-d-death? A-a-are y-you -s-serious?" William stuttered.

"Don't worry mate. It won't be that long. I reckon it will be a maximum of 1 week. We will die due to starvation and dehydration."

"That is not what I want to hear."

"That is the truth. We are stuck here."

Right then, James felt something in his coat.

"Wait a second. Is this a key?"

"WHERE DID YOU GET THIS FROM?"

"I don't know. OH! It was dangling on the tree in the backyard of the castle."

"THIS COULD BE IT. GIVE IT TO ME."

He used the key to try and unlock the door and sure enough it opened.

"WE HAVE DONE IT" Yelled William

"YES! THIS IS THE TIME FOR OUR REVENGE."

"Let us go to the castle quick!"

"Yes."

As they went out, they saw a passerby. They decided to ask him about the date.

"Good day, sir. Do you know what day is it today?"

"Oh, it's January 1st, 1899."

"Thank you, sir. Do you know what is the time right now?"

"It is currently 15 past 11."

Thank you, sir."

"You are welcome, gentlemen."

"William, this means that we were stuck here for the past 1 week."

"How did the time go so fast?"

"I don't know. But now, we have to get to the castle as soon as possible. We have to capture them. Something sinister is going on."

"Yeah, there it is, the mansion." Said William.

"Hide behind those bushes in the backyard. If they find us, we could be in big trouble."

"Ok, James."

They hid behind the bushes for more than an hour until they saw the fake Rudolph, the fake Catherine, and the Fake Rutherford going towards the garden. They listened to what they said but didn't get any clue related to them. They decided to buy a gas bomb and drop it in the garden to confuse them. This will give them the time to cover their noses with a special chemical which will make them unconscious. Then they will carry them toward the room in which they were trapped and lock them. James discussed this plan with William and he thought that it was a good idea. He volunteered to buy the bomb and the chemical from the nearby store which sold weapons which was usually for the rich. James said that he had to pretend that he was a member of the family which owned the mansion. James also told him to tell the shopkeeper that he would pay the due money later. James also said that he would be keeping an eye on them.

After that, William quietly exited the yard and made his

way to the store. He quickly bought the things and returned to the backyard."

"Here it is James."

"Good."

"Where are they right now?"

"Right in that garden. Quick, follow me silently. Drop this bomb near to them when I say so."

"Okay"

As they reached the garden, William threw the gas bomb right at their feet when James gave him the sign. As the bomb produced a thick cloud, no one was able to see anything. Somehow, James managed to poison them with the chemical.

"YES! They are now unconscious. We now have an hour until they wake up."

"But how will we carry them to the building without causing any suspicions?"

"Using a cycle?"

"How?"

"Just watch me do it"

He was able to carry the bodies one by one to the building on the cycle by laying the bodies on his back. He then proceeded to tie their hands and legs to prevent them from escaping somehow. This method prevented any suspicions from the passersby and was also efficient.

"How was that, William?"

"It was smart, James. How do you even come up with this kind of solution?"

"Just my brain."

"Hahaha"

"Anyway, get on the cycle quick. We have to go to the building as soon as possible. They will wake up any second now."

"Sure, let us go."

They reached the building in 10 minutes, just in time to close the huge iron door, which prevented them from going out. The loud sound woke them up, and they were confused as to where they were being held.

CHAPTER 10:

THE

INTERROGATION

"Where are we?" Asked the fake Rudolph.

"This is the place where we imprison our victims. How did we get here?"

"I don't have any idea. I remember standing in the garden and now we are kneeling at the camp." Said 'Rutherford'

Right then, James opened the small vent through which he could speak.

"Well, well, well."

"How did you get out? Why are we stuck here?" asked 'Rudolph'

"Calm down monsters. I will tell you everything. I will not make you wait for an entire just like you did to us."

"Let us out?"

"No. First of all, let me tell you how we escaped."

"Please tell them." Said William in a mocking tone.

"Right as we were leaving the mansion on Christmas day, I saw a key dangling on the tree. I took it without anyone else noticing and kept it in my coat. After we were locked in inside the room, due to anxiety I just forgot all about this. I remembered that I had a key on New Year's Day, which is today. William unlocked the door and we were free. We had our food and then came to the mansion to capture you. I reckon you remember the white smoke just before you passed. That was due to a smoke bomb. Then I used some chemicals to make you sleep. I carried your bodies on cycle till here. I hope this is enough. Now I demand an explanation from you. Why did you bring us here and what are your motives?”

“We will not tell you.” Yelled Catherine.

“Is that so? No problem! We will make you speak.”

“How do you plan to do so?

“Using torture, maybe.”

“You can’t.

“You simply cannot.”

“WE WILL. We will take the revenge. You have until tomorrow morning to confess or we will resort to torture. And we will not feed you until you confess. Is that clear?”

No one replied to him. This infuriated James, so he closed the vent.

"Alright then. Suffer."

"Do you think they will confess the truth, or just make up some make-believe?"

"No, they will not confess that easily. But I will make them confess."

"How?"

"Using torture."

"Isn't that a little bit too extreme?"

"No. Compared to what we had to suffer through for the past 2 weeks; this is going to be nothing."

"What do we do now? Return to our hotel room?"

"Yes. But I reckon that we booked the room for only 5 days, but today marks the 9th day. We have to speak with the manager and sort it out."

"Ok, James."

They reached their hotel within 15 minutes and they both entered with a tense face wondering whether the manager would even let them in. But they sighed a sigh of relief when he let them in. But the manager was suspicious.

"Phew! Didn't think that he would let us in."

"Yeah"

"Anyway, I am extremely hungry right now. I seriously want some food."

"Me too. Let us go to the local pizzeria."

"Sure let us go. I want a relief from these adventures."

They had their food at the pizzeria and returned to their hotel.

"I wonder what the monsters are doing right now in their dungeon."

"Probably suffering, Hahahaha. Anyway, I am going to take a long nap. I am too tired from all these shenanigans."

"Me too"

 James and William decided to take a nap but they were surprised when they woke only the next day morning.

"Blimey! I reckon we slept for 18 hours straight." Exclaimed William.

There was no reply from James as he was still half asleep.

"Wake up James. We have to go to the mortuary.

"Oh right. Let us go without wasting any more time."

They got ready and reached the building just in time as the 3 of them woke up.

"Well, Good morning. Any plans on confessing?"

"No, James. We will not tell anything even if you kill one of us."

"Oh really, then get ready Rudolph for your death within an hour."

"No! Please don't kill me. I am just a child."

"Yes. You are a child. THE CHILD OF A DEMON." Screamed William.

"Calm down, William."

"You will not be able to make us confess. Just quit already." Said Rutherford.

"Never. A detective never quits so easily. I will never leave this place until you confess. Is that clear? You have got an hour before I start to torture you."

"What are you going to use?" asked William.

"Acids!"

"Where did you get these from?"

"I bought these yesterday. Hahaha."

At this point, the fake Catherine, Rudolph, and Rutherford were getting extremely tense. But they know, that if they confess, a larger problem will be awaiting them. As a result, they kept mum for the entire 1 hour.

"Well, well, well. An hour has passed. No plans to confess yet?"

The three of them kept mum.

"Oh, I see. Keeping mum will not do anything. Open up or I will resort to violence."

Again, disobeying him, they kept mum.

"Ok, that is it. William, come with me inside. Let's start the torture session. Hahahaha. Come here, Rudolph. Oh, sorry. I forgot that I had tied your legs and arms. No worries. I will come near you."

William realized that this wasn't the same James that he met back at Old London 15 years back. He was more furious and violent now due to his sufferings. William realized that James had gone mad.

Right then, before William could stop James, he poured the acid right on Rudolph's face. He cried in pain as the acid slowly dissolved his skin. The pain was too much to handle but still didn't confess.

"Ahh, you are a strong man. But I will not stop until one of you confess."

He again poured the acid but this time in his mouth. This dissolved Rudolph's tongue and some parts of his esophagus.

"No, no stop. I will tell you. But please stop. I cannot take this anymore. Please stop. Mom, please tell them the secret. I will not be able to endure this once again. Please, Mom."

"No son. We have to respect the wishes of our lord."

"Lord? Who is your lord, Catherine?"

"I will not tell you."

"Well, it seems like, I will pour this on your face then."

"Please no!"

"Only, if you confess."

"We will not."

"Okay."

James then proceeded to pour the acid all over her face. She screamed in agony as he poured a large amount of the acid.

"Stop it! Please stop. I will tell you. Please stop."

"Don't confess Emmeline. Please don't." Said the fake Rutherford.

"Well, I guess one more person deserves the acid. Hahaha"

No, no, no. Don't pour the acid, please. We will tell you."

"No, it will be unfair right?" asked James as he poured the acid on his face.

"Ahhh!"

"Let this be a lesson for you to not mess up with a detective. Now confess everything that you are hiding from us."

"We need some water and food. Please."

"Sure. Here it is. I brought this for us just in case. Now freshen up and get to the point quickly."

The 3 of them used almost all of their water to wash their face to get some relief from the pain that they were going through. Then they had some food.

"Ok. I hope you all have freshened up. Now, get to the point."

"Ok."

"I will ask you some questions and you need to answer them honestly. Do NOT make things up. Or else you shall suffer. Is that clear?"

"Yes"

Ok then, first of all, reveal your identities and background, Catherine."

"We are the Fletcher family. I am Emmeline, Rudolph's actual name is Richard and Rutherford goes by the name of Rutherford.

"Ok. Interesting. Why do you pretend to be the Deadwood family?"

"This is a long story."

"That is not a problem. I have got all day."

"20 years back, we were captured by a drug smuggler from Australia. We were camping in Australia on our honeymoon in Brisbane on that fateful night when someone assaulted us and took us to a mysterious building. We were held captive in that building and we were trained by him to capture detectives from all over the world."

"What was his intent?"

"He aimed to bring all those people to the building a perform a surgery to remove their brains."

"Why would he even want to do that?"

"He intended to mash all those brains and create a potion out of it and sell it in the black market."

"Has he done that?"

"No, you were intended to be his last victim."

"How many detectives are there in total?"

"99. 27 from Australia, 10 from England, 15 from USA, 31 from Spain and 16 from Russia."

"A wide variety indeed. Are all those people still alive?"

"Yes. They have been deep frozen and he intends to melt them after we have successfully captured all 100 detectives."

"Do you know the exact location?"

"No. But it is somewhere in Brisbane. If I am right, then the building should be as tall as a 3-story building. It was painted with a faint brown color."

"I am pretty sure that you have the exact coordinates."

"No, we don't."

"Well, what is that is that in your pocket? Give it to me. Oh, well I am right. These are the exact coordinates."

"Yes. You are right."

"Anyway, what is his name? Also, are you forced by him?"

"His name is Philip Johnson. He had threatened to kill us if we leaked his identity."

"Good. Thank you for your cooperation. I have many more questions to ask you, but now you can take some rest."

"Can we go outside?"

"No."

After he locked the room, he signaled William to follow him to the hotel. After they reached their hotel room, they had a deep conversation.

"So, they were doing this due to desperation," said William.

"I am feeling a little guilty about pouring Sulfuric acid on their faces." Said, James

"Poor family. We must help the trapped 99 detectives to escape from there."

"Why did you stop the interrogation? You could have got even more information, right?"

"I couldn't help myself but get too guilty. That is the reason why. I wasn't the same person then. I feel like something changed in me. I am not the kind of person who finds pleasure in others' suffering. I am not sadistic. But today was an exception. That betrayal had gotten into my mind. I was expecting to get the revenge for all of our sufferings."

"Well, the damage that you have done is permanent. That scar that formed on their faces after you poured the acid is permanent. They are done for life. Especially that young kid. I believe that he could have had a bright future if you hadn't destroyed his face." Replied William.

"I don't know what to do now. I am feeling low. I just want to end my life."

"No, please don't say that."

"I am just going to take a nap. I have got nothing else to do." Said James with a teary eye.

He went to bed but he was not able to sleep due to the guilt.

"I am not even able to sleep."

"No problem. Let us go to the building and ask some more questions,"

"Mm. Okay."

James was unwilling to visit the mortuary once again, but he had to. He had to save those poor 99 scientists stuck in Brisbane. After he reached the mortuary, he opened the room and started talking with them. He genuinely wanted to apologize to them. But he didn't due to his ego.

"Well, I am here to ask the rest of the questions. Are you ready?"

"Yes."

"Okay. 2 weeks back, you had sent me the mail to come to Hellingwood, right? Why were you not able to come to Old London by yourselves?"

"We were the residents of Old London. So, if someone recognized me then, it could cause a lot of problems."

"Why did you bring us to Deadwood? You would have been able to capture us at Hellingwood itself, right?"

"On that day, Richard and Rutherford were from Brisbane after they captured Sir. Charles Wellington. I wouldn't have been able to do it alone."

"Ok. That explains this a lot. Were you the person who added Mercury to our food back at Hellingwood?"

"Yes, but that was an accident. I meant to add vinegar."

"Why did you have Mercury with you?"

"Oh, it was actually from the 97th heist back in Moscow."

"Who did you kidnap in Moscow?"

"Vladimir Neskrans"

"Ok. While we were traveling from Hellingwood to Deadwood, we were subjected to different attacks. Who did that?"

"It was Richard."

"Mm, okay. Whose mansion did you use to trick us?"

"It was our lord's old castle."

"When we entered the taxi, I saw you smirking at the driver. Who was he?"

"It was Rutherford."

"Oh! Ok.

"Lastly, why did you hesitate to let us go to the backyard of the mansion?"

"That is where the bombs were stored. Luckily, Rutherford hid it in time."

"Where did he hide them?"

"Right behind the old banyan tree."

"Okay. So that is it. That is the very end of the interrogation. Thank you very much for cooperating with us."

"So, what will you two do with this much information?"

"We will go to Brisbane tomorrow itself."

"What about us? Will we stay in here forever?"

"No, we will give you a month's worth of rations today. We will free you once we return."

"But what if you don't return?"

"We would surely return. Don't worry about that."

"But there is one problem: this project's deadline is on the 13th. On the 14th, he will kill all those 99 people and create the potion. He will not wait for you."

"Thanks for telling me this. Goodbye."

James then went to the local market and bought the ration for them. After that, they returned to their rooms.

"Quite exhausting day today. Isn't it?" Asked William.

"Sure, it is. Get ready to go to Brisbane tomorrow."

"But how?"

"I have booked a ferry from here to the capital of Travancore. And from there, a ferry would take us to Brisbane."

"That must have cost a fortune."

"Yes, it did. But we have to make some sacrifices for the greater good."

"Anyway, what is the time right now?"

"My watch says that it is currently 6 pm."

"When is our ferry tomorrow?"

"10 am."

"So we have to get ready for the long journey. How long will it take us to reach Brisbane?"

"About 25 days. Anyway, our train is scheduled to depart at 7 pm. So let us go"

"Ok then. Let us go!"

"Let me call a taxi."

CHAPTER 11
JOURNEY TO BRISBANE

They walked to the Deadwood station and then boarded the train just as it departed.

"Oh my lord, that was a close one. The train almost left without us." Said William.

"Yeah."

"How long will it take us to reach The Hague?"

"About 15 hours."

"That means we will reach the station at 10 am. But our ferry is also supposed to depart at 10 am. There is no gap between them. It will take us about 30 minutes to reach the seaport. That means we will MISS the ferry."

"Oh goodness gracious me, I didn't think about this! What will we do now? The next train to Travancore only departs 2 weeks later."

"Oh no!"

"I hope something miraculous happens tomorrow."

"Yeah. Anyway, we can see what happens tomorrow."

By the Lord's mercy, they reached 45 minutes before the actual time.

"Thank you, Lord, for helping us. We will be highly indebted to you." Said James.

"Quick, call a taxi. We have to go to the seaport as soon as possible."

Right then, he saw a taxi driver.

"Hey sir, can you drop us at the seaport?"

"Sure, get inside."

They reached the port within 40 minutes. They boarded the ship just as it left the shore.

"Oh lord, this is the 2nd time in a row when we almost missed our vehicle."

"Yeah."

"Oh, I forgot to tell you that I am seasick." Said, William

"It doesn't matter, as the only way to go to Brisbane is by boarding a ship."

Shortly after they reached the ocean, a huge storm frightened the passengers. But the attendants tried to calm them by saying that this was just a small wave and wouldn't cause any damage.

"Oh lord, look at those waves. Will we drown today?"

"No." Said, James

"I hope we reach Travancore as quickly as possible without dying."

The storm continued for the next 2 hours, and it stopped eventually. As the storm was a bit strong, the ship was forced to move at a slow pace. This wasted their time and as a result, they reached Travancore a whopping 9 hours late. The ship to Brisbane was scheduled to depart 4 hours before they reached Travancore. As a result, they missed their ferry.

"Oh no! What will we do now? The next ship to Brisbane is 3 days later. We are stuck here for 3 days then. We cannot afford to be late"

"We don't even know the local language. How will we communicate with others?"

"Don't worry. This is a British colony, so there must be a British general somewhere out here. Let us search for one."

"Ok."

CHAPTER 12: TALKING WITH THE COMMANDER

After hours of wandering, they finally met a British general. They introduced themselves and then told their problem.

"Oh, hello there sir. Good morning" Greeted James

"Good morning gentlemen. What brings you here, gentlemen?"

"We are detectives from Great Britain. We are stranded here as we missed our connecting ship to Brisbane for our next case."

"Oh, interesting. Well, I am Sir. Edward Seymour. Anyway, follow me to my residence. We can talk about this, there. I want to know more about yourselves."

"Oh thank you, sir."

After walking for 10 minutes through the narrow roads made of mud, they finally reached the official residence of the man. By the looks of the building, it looked like the residence of the high commanding general of the British army.

"I reckon that you are a general in the British army." Said William.

"Specifically, the commander of the British Navy."

"Oh wow." Exclaimed William.

James and William were both awe-struck when they entered the huge palace. The building was adorned with marble of the best quality, beautiful shiny diamonds, and jewelry made of gold and silver. It was truly a mansion of the heavens. They were so awes struck by this, that they could not reply when the general called them.

"Oh well, I reckon these peasants have not seen anything like this before." Muttered the general to himself

"I wish we lived in a palace like this."

"Hahaha. Do you fancy some food?"

"Sure."

They sat down at their table and started talking while the food was being served by the servants.

"So tell me more about yourselves and your case."

"Sure sire. So first of all, let me introduce myself. I am James Faulkner and my companion is William Shorteye. We were the residents of old London."

"Oh right. Well, I am actually from a place which is a little far away – Hellingwood."

"WHAT?! Really?"

"Yeah. What is so surprising about it?"

"About 20 days ago, we received a weird letter. It was full of code inside. We somehow decoded the letter within an hour and it instructed us to go to the local pub at Hellingwood the next day by 8:00 am."

"Oh, it is quite interesting. Tell me more about this."

"Sure. I reckon it will take a long time to explain the whole incident. So I will try to shorten the story a bit."

"No problem. Hahaha"

"We reached the Hellingwood station the next day 30 minutes past 8.00 am. We were late by 30 minutes, so I quickly ran outside the station and entered the bar which was just opposite the railway station. William was not able to come with me because he injured his leg while jumping from the train. Inside, I found a woman sitting in a dark corner of the bar. Her name was supposedly Catherine."

"What do you mean by 'supposedly'?"

"You will find out later in this story."

"Okay then, please continue."

"As I was saying, I found the lady sitting at the corner of the bar. She saw me standing at the entrance and invited me to come and serve myself a drink. As a non-drinker, I politely refused and started interrogating her. But she insisted that we wait until my companion, William arrived."

"How did she know that William was injured?"

"She probably had a spy or two at the station. Who knows?"

"Oh, interesting."

"Anyway, after William arrived at the bar, she covered his would with a cloth and offered him a drink. He refused as he was also a non–drinker. Then I asked her about the letter and the actual case. She answered that her sister Juliana Deadwood was murdered back at their home place. But this all turned out to be a big lie. But when we realized it, it was too late.

After the interrogation though, she took us to her house for breakfast. It was a tasty English breakfast, but unbeknownst to us, the food was poisoned with Mercury."

"What happened next, gentlemen?"

"After about 30 minutes, we started feeling sick and nauseous. It was so bad that even the 'Catherine' was sick.

We took a sample to the nearby lab and discovered it was poisoned with pure Mercury."

"Do you know who was behind this?"

"It was Catherine."

'How? As you told me, Catherine ate the poisoned food and got sick herself. No person who wants to poison others would want to poison themselves right?"

"That was the same reason why we didn't suspect her."

"So, was the entire case just fake and just an attempt to kill you men?"

"Yes. But we realized this way too late in the story."

"Please resume the story. I am curious."

"Ok. So, we departed from Hellingwood Station to the Deadwood Station the next day. There was not a direct train to Deadwood Station, therefore, I reckon we traveled in 3 trains and one ferry. And a lot of things happened that should have alerted us that she was an evil force. But unfortunately, it never did,"

"What do you mean by that?"

"There were explosions, death and so much, all planned by an evil force at Brisbane. I don't want to explain everything that happened that day, as it was tragic. Many people were killed in an attempt to capture us. Even after all these incidents, it never hit me that, our client was the person who was instructed to do all this."

"No worries, mate. You can skip to the next part."

"After we reached Deadwood, she took us to the Deadwood castle. But as we entered the taxi, I saw something which made me suspicious of Catherine for the first time."

"What was it, mate?"

"I saw her winking and smirking at the taxi driver."

"What is so unusual about that?"

"I don't know. But I had an eerie feeling about her for the first time."

"Mm, okay."

"Due to this eerie feeling, I refused to stay at the palace for the night. I told her that we would be staying at the nearby hotel. I did not reply to her questions as I was deep in thought. I do not remember what I was thinking but it was certainly related to the incidents that happened in the past few days. "

"What happened next, mate?"

After we arrived at the hotel, I locked all the windows and doors of the room. I also covered the cracks in the wall with a cloth and then turned off all the lights and then took a nap."

"Mm. What happened the next day?"

"The next day we woke up early in the morning and went to the castle. To our surprise, Catherine and the castle's 2 security guards were standing just near the gate. They welcomed us in and then I started the investigation."

"There must have been no clues in the castle right as the murder was just a story?"

"You are right. There were no actual clues, but there were many setups in the castle."

"Like what?"

"Like broken glass which we found in the kitchen and human hair which was kept close to the place where the apparent 'murder' took place."

"Oh really. What happened next?"

"The incident which happened next was intriguing."

"What was it?"

"As we were climbing down the stairs, we saw the shadow of someone behind the windows. When I asked Catherine about it, she tried to play it off by saying it was just probably a security guard. But I knew it was not."

"How do you know that."

"The shadow was significantly taller than the security guards which we found at the front gate. So I quickly went out to check, but there was no one. Right then, Catherine suggested that we should go to the mortuary where the dead body was stored. Right as we were leaving, I found a key dangling on the tree. I took it and hid it in my coat without anyone noticing. Before long, we reached the mortuary. However, the building that she claimed was a mortuary where Juliana's body was stored was quite unusual."

"Why do you think that it was unusual?"

"There were a few reasons to justify my suspicions. Firstly there was no graveyard behind or anywhere near the building. Also, the building looked odd as it had no windows or doors other than the front door."

"Oh, okay. What happened next?"

"Upon entering the office, we encountered Mr. Rutherford, whom Catherine identified as the mortician. I asked him several questions about the body, but it was evident that he was quite irritated by my persistent inquiries. Additionally, he was rather rude in his responses. Then Catherine led me to the room where she claimed Juliana's body was stored. Suddenly, I realized something crucial."

"What was it?"

"I remembered that Catherine had told me that her sister was murdered 15 days ago. On average a human body takes about 10 days to decompose. So there was absolutely no chance that the body was intact even if the body was stored in cold conditions. Right when I was about to ask Catherine about this, she locked us in with the help of a huge iron wall. It took us about a week to get out of there. We thought that we were stuck here until our death."

"How did you escape then?"

"It is a long story. Catherine promised to free us the next day, but we were stuck in the dungeon for 6 to 7 days. We started to hallucinate due to the lack of water and food. We didn't know the passing of time as my clock was not adjusted to the local time. We were blind in that room. Finally, after 7 days I felt something in my coat. It was the key I took without anyone's knowledge 7 days back. William knew that it was the key to our freedom. He tried to unlock the door, and sure enough, it opened."

"What did you do next?"

"We knew that we had to take revenge for our sufferings. So we went straight toward the

Deadwood Castle to check on them. About 10 minutes after we reached the castle, we saw them entering the garden. We hid behind the bushes to try and hear what they were speaking, but it was useless. I instructed William to go to the nearby store and buy a smoke bomb and some poison."

"Why? What was your plan?"

"We planned to throw the smoke bomb at their feet which will create huge smoke and as a result, they will not be able to see anything. We would take advantage of those precious seconds to apply some poison to their faces which will cause them to sleep for 1 hour. Then I would carry the bodies to the office on a bicycle and then trap them in the room in which we had been stuck for the past 1 week. And, we were successful in this."

"So are they still in the room?"

"Yes."

"When do you plan to free them?"

"After we capture the main head of the scheme for which they have trained and brainwashed to work for."

"Who is that?"

"We will get to that shortly sir."

"Ok. Go on then."

"So, after they woke up, we started the interrogation. They refused to confess anything but that was until I poured some acid on their faces-."

"EXCUSE ME! WHAT? You poured acid all over their faces?!"

"I am sorry but I had to do it. I had no other choice."

"Ok then, tell me what happened during the interrogation."

"Ok."

"During the interrogation, we learned their real names. Catherine's real name was Emmeline Fletcher, Rudolph was Richard and the mortician was Rutherford."

"Do you know what were their intentions?"

"Yes, they planned to capture me and take me to Brisbane to present me to their lord."

"Who is their lord and why do they intend to capture you?"

"It was Philip Johnson. He-"

"WAIT A SECOND. PHILIP JOHNSON?!"

"Yes. What is so surprising about this?"

"He is our number one target."

"Why so?"

"For the past, like 15 years we have been getting cases of detectives and intellectuals getting kidnapped from all around the world. In all those cases Philip Johnson was evident."

"How?"

"He used to write his and the victim's name as a code at the victim's house. We had finally decoded it last year, and sure enough it was Philip Johnson and his 99 other victims. I reckon that you were about to be his 100th. But the thing is, we don't know why he keeps on kidnapping detectives."

"Well, I have the answer to it. We got it during the interrogation."

"What is it, mate?"

"Emmeline told me that after I am sent to him, he will melt the others and me, and then he will kill them, taking away their brains to create a potion. The reason for this is unclear. She told me that the deadline for this project is on the 13th of January. So if we are late to stop him, he will not wait for my arrival and then kill all those souls to achieve his goals."

"Well say no more, gentlemen. I am with you in this mission. This mission is personal to me as I had also lost my young brother to him. We shall take revenge and save those poor 99 souls. We will depart today itself."

"But wait, sir. The next ship to Brisbane is 3 days later. How will we reach there in time?"

"I reckon you forgot that I am the commander of the British Navy. I have the entire fleet waiting for my command. We shall depart Travancore for Brisbane tonight. I will order 2 of my high-ranking soldiers to come with me too. Come, follow me to my office upstairs."

"Yes sir."

They soon arrived at his office. He signaled a soldier to call his 2 high-ranking generals, and soon enough, the generals arrived.

"Vice Admiral Nelson Horiato reporting, sir!"

"Vice Admiral William Moriarty reporting, sir!"

"Good morning, gentlemen. I have got some duty for you."

"Yes sir!" They both said it at the same time.

"Tonight we will be departing for Brisbane for a case. Prepare the submarine as quickly as possible. You both will be coming with us. Is that clear?"

"Yes sir!"

"Good. So get ready lads. We will be departing for Brisbane tonight." He said to William and James"

"But how?"

"With the best and the most advanced submarine in the British navy. This submarine is specifically reserved for me."

"Oh, I have never been on a submarine before. But I am pretty sure that the submarine has limited space in it right?" Asked William

"Yes. What is the problem mate?"

"Uhh, I am highly claustrophobic. So this won't be a cakewalk for me."

"That doesn't matter, William. Don't think about yourselves.

Think about the 99 souls that we are about to rescue in a few days. That should provide you with enough confidence, right?"

"Yes, James."

Right then one of the vice admirals came to the office with a grim face.

"What is the issue, Nelson?"

"Sir. We expect a perilous storm in the Andaman and Nicobar Islands. This could cause a possible tsunami. It will be perilous for us."

"Don't care. We have to reach there without wasting a single second. Nelson, when do you think we will reach the city of Brisbane?"

"Accounting for the possible storm, it will take us about 11 days."

"What?!" exclaimed William.

"If we leave today, then I reckon we will reach on the 13th."

"Oh no. January 13th is the deadline. We would be too late then."

"Let us hope for the best." Said James.

"Well, let us not waste any more time, let us leave. Nelson, prepare the crew. We are leaving now."

"Yes sir!"

"James and William, follow me."

"Ok, sir."

Within 10 minutes, they reached the private sea port, where the submarine and its crew were waiting for them.

"Welcome onboard, sir."

"Thank you. Well, let us then, you know, start the engines and depart for Brisbane as soon as possible, Nelson"

"Sure sir."

"This is super crammed up in here. I am having difficulty in breathing. How do soldiers even sit in here, James?"

"They are pretty tough people."

"That is right. I remember being crammed up in a submarine during the British and French battles many years back. Ah, I recall my days of glory being a soldier."

"Nice."

"Well then, take your seats and strap your seatbelts. It is going to be a perilous journey."

"Will we die?" Asked William.

"Of course, not. We are professionals in this matter."

"I hope so."

Right then, the crew started the submarine propellers and were off to Brisbane. It was a smooth ride, and before they knew it, it was midnight. They planned to rest at Moluccas Island for the night. But nobody could have expected what would happen next.

"Well lads, it is too dangerous to continue our journey due to the high waves. We are quite close to Moluccas Island, so we will rest there for the night and depart tomorrow early in the morning. Is that okay gentleman?"

"Perfectly okay" Replied James.

"Well then Moriarty, instruct Nelson to stop at the Moluccas Island."

"Ok, sir."

In just five minutes, they arrived at the shore of Moluccas Island. The island looked as pleasant as ever, but little did they know that something or someone dangerous awaited them.

"Ahh, what a beautiful and quiet island it is. Just as the history books described it as." Exclaimed Nelson

"True that." Agreed Moriarty.

"Okay, Enough chit-chatting. Set up your tents and sleep. We have to depart early tomorrow."

"Right as they started setting up their tents, they heard something. It was a cry of a person. They realized that they were not alone on this island. It was the cry of a tribesman alerting others.

"Oh lord, what was that?" Sir. Edward thought to himself.

"Oh look there! An army of tribesmen. They are armed with spears. They are dangerous. Run! Run away!" screamed William.

"Oh goodness gracious me. He is right. Everyone, please retreat to the submarine as fast as possible. Leave behind the tents.

Save your life." Screamed Sir Edward to everyone.

Right then, the tallest person in the army of tribesmen shot an arrow towards them. Unfortunately, it hit James, right on his right arm.

"Ahh. It is paining."

"Are you alright mate?" Asked William.

"Yes, I am fine. Now run fast to the submarine. I will follow you."

Fortunately, all five of them entered the submarine without injuries and safely departed the island.

"Quick, Moriarty. Bring the first aid. We have to cover James's wound as soon as possible."

"Ok, sir. Here it is."

Sir Edward quickly applied the medicine and then covered his wound.

"How are you feeling mate?" Asked Sir Edward

"Fine. Thank you mate for helping me out."

"No worries, James."

11 DAYS LATER..............

Have we reached Brisbane yet?" Asked William in a sleepy tone

"Not yet. I reckon it will take an hour more."

"Oh lord, I reckon today's the deadline for Philip's killing spree. How will we find his office, mate? Brisbane's a huge city, mind you." Exclaimed James

"Poor people. You got any plans, James?"

"No."

"Ah no."

"Do not worry. I will save them."

"How?"

"You will see."

CHAPTER 13:

ANSWERS AT LAST:

An hour passed. It was now 8.44 am. As soon as they reached the shore, they signaled a taxi to pick them up.

"Good morning, mate. Where are you off to?" Asked the taxi driver.

"Well, we are not sure."

"What do you mean? Reckon you are a tourist?"

"No, mate. Here are the coordinates. Please take us there."

"Sure sire."

"Thank you."

"Mind if I tell you, this place is located on the outskirts of the city? It will cost you a lot."

"No worries, mate. I will pay."
Said Sir Edward

"Well, then we are off."

"How long will it take to reach the address?"

"About an hour."

"That's good."

An hour passed and they finally reached the destination, or at least according to the driver.

"Ok then, we have reached."

"Is this the correct place? I don't see anyone or anything here."

"Well, I don't know. Good luck with whatever you are trying to do."

"Thanks, man."

"Oh, don't forget my 38$"

"Yeah, here it is."

"Thank you, sir. Have a great day ahead."

"You too."

By this time, everyone was in a good mood. They expected to capture the culprit and send him to England. But it was not going to be as easy as they thought. And unbeknownst to anyone, a greater danger loomed before James.

"There is absolutely nothing over here. It is a barren land. Did he fool us, mate?" Asked William

"I don't know. Let us explore this place for any clues."

They searched for a while, but their efforts were in vain. After a while, something no one could have expected happened. William, while walking around mindlessly, stepped on a red button. This caused the ground beneath him to crack open, sending him falling through a pipe.

"No, William!" James exclaimed with horror."

"This is a trap. I reckon we have reached Philip's hiding spot." Said Sir. Edward.

"How will we save him?"

"Should we jump in?"

"Not. We would all get stuck in his jail."

"Then how would we get inside?"

"Since the trap is here, the main entrance should be somewhere in this area."

"Quick, my soldiers. Find the entrance."

"Yes sir."

"Yes sir!"

"Very well, my soldiers."

Before long, Sir Edward himself found a suspicious metal manhole, hidden by a bunch of bushes.

"Oh well, mate. I reckon I have found the entrance."

"Very well sir."

"Nelson and Moriarty, please open this."

"No, they can't do that."

"Why, do you doubt my soldiers' ability?"

"No sir. They simply cannot open this with their strength."

"Why?"

"If you look carefully, you can see a metal lock on the manhole. It has also got some numbers on it. It is a hi-tech lock."

"How will we open this?"

"Let me think. Wait a second. Remember the bomb explosions which I told you back in India?"

"Yeah, what about it?"

"When we examined the fragments, we found some text on it."

"What were they mate?"

"I reckon there were 2. - 'MADE IN DEADWOOD' and a code.

But I don't remember the exact number."

"That might be it. Think harder, mate."

"Uhh, I am pretty sure that it was a 6-digit number. Uhh, what was it?"

"You got it, mate."

"YES! I got it. Let me try 270125. YES!! IT UNLOCKED."

"Well done mate. Let us then enter the manhole."

"Sure."

James, Nelson, Moriarty, and Sir Edward climbed down the stairs through the dark and gloomy hole to reach a huge room. There was no one inside. It was eerily silent. Suddenly, a creepy laugh broke the silence.

"Hey, who is that?" Asked William.

"Well, well, well. My 100th victim has arrived."

"Who are you?"

"Hahaha. I am pretty sure that you know me. I am Philip Johnson."

"Yes. I know you."

"Turn on the lights, guards. Let them see the 100 prisoners over there."

"Yes, Your Majesty."

The guards turned on the lights to honor his order. Just as they could see clearly, they saw the victims, all frozen in time waiting for their deaths. James then saw something, which broke his heart. William screaming for his life.

"Free them. Why would you want to hold them hostage?"

"I have got reasons for that, and I am sure that you are aware of them. To extract their brain and sell them in the black market."

"Why would you want to sell them? Who would even buy them?"

"My loyal customers. They have been waiting for me for the last 15 years and today is the last day. Hahaha"

"Free them, or else you will face the consequences."

"Guards, capture them. They are too ambitious. My machine is ready. It is hungry for their brains. Hahaha."

"Stop that at once." Screamed James as the guards tried to assault them."

"Fire!" Screamed Sir Edward.

"At that moment, the sound of bullets could be heard. The cries of the wounded guards."

"No! My servants. How dare you. Attack them." Screamed Philip.

Within a few seconds, an army of soldiers surrounded them. James somehow escaped from them, with the guards knowing. He hid behind the walls and watched miserably as his comrades were taken away by the guards.

"No. What will I do now? I am alone in this journey."

"Where is James?!" Screamed Philip, when his guards presented him with the new captures.

"Oh, we are sorry sir, but it seems that James has escaped from us."

"No, it is not possible for anyone to leave this room without my knowledge. He is hiding somewhere in this room. Quick, go and find him."

"Yes sir."

Unaware of the danger, James sat there sulking.

"Nooo! My friends are gone. My family is gone. I am a lonely man."

Right then, one of the guards saw him sitting behind the pillar near the storage room.

"There you are. You will be dead any second now."

"No, no, nooo!" James cried in pain and horror, as he was dragged away to the center of the room, where he could see everything: Philip, the guards, his comrades, and the 99 other intellectuals.

"Tie him up. We don't want him to escape."

"As you say, sir."

"Well then James, I have realized that your brain is not comparable to those of the 99 other detectives combined. You are the person I wanted for 15 years. You are a genius. I have a condition for you, then."

"Please continue."

"If you agree to sacrifice yourselves, then, I shall release all my prisoners without killing them. Is that okay?"

James looked around the room, tensed. He saw the frowned faces of the detectives and his comrades awaiting their death. Then, with a heavy heart, he said: "Yes."

"Very well then. Guards shoot him and then take him to the room, and perform the necessary procedures."

'Yes sir."

Right at that moment, in front of everyone's eyes, he was shot........

"Noooooo!" William screamed in terror as his old friend fell to the ground, soulless.....

"Guards, release the prisoners and escort them to their hotels, safely."

"Ok, sir."

William was not given the chance to see his friend's body. This broke his heart. Seeing this, Sir Edward tried to console him."

"Don't worry William. I am sure that he is immensely pleased with himself for saving others. In honor of his bravery, January 13th shall be celebrated as World Selflessness Day throughout the world until the end of time."

There was nothing William could do. He returned to England and stayed at the hut where he used to until he died due to Pneumonia 18 years later. As for Philip Johnson, he was captured by the British army on the 7th of July 1901, after an intense search..........

ABOUT THE AUTHOR

V.S. Aravindh is a 7th-grade student who loves writing exciting mystery stories. He has a passion for solving puzzles and exploring history, which he often combines in his writing. When he's not writing, Aravindh enjoys reading books, drinking tea, and playing games that challenge his mind. *The Murder at the Deadwood Castle* is his very first novel, filled with twists, secrets, and thrilling adventures. Aravindh hopes to write many more stories that will keep readers on the edge of their seats.

Support the author!

SUBSCRIBE!